The Adventures of
Starla Cascade:
Space Hooker

The God in the
Machine

Eli Grant

To Mike and Jeremy. You turned me on to robots, and now robots turn me on. Thanks.

When Starla was small, she had often dreamed of flying. Arms spread, hair a red banner behind her, she glided on the wind above a world she'd never seen. She grazed the tree tops of a lush and alien forest, knocking the dew from flowers too fantastic to exist in life, startling flocks of winged creatures with eyes like living gemstones and feathers that shimmered in iridescent rainbows. She swooped through the ruins of a crumbling pyramid, walls still painted with the intricate and esoteric symbolism of its forgotten masters even as they were consumed by the flowering moss, and within the temple's dark interior strange and ageless beasts were chained, still guarding tombs where golden treasure sat falling into dust. She flew above a vast and glittering city, diving into the canyon of its magnificent buildings to sweep along the ever turning river of its streets, passing people both fair and foul living out complex little lives she couldn't conceive of. Soaring above strange landscapes, she had felt invulnerable, far from the reach of anything that could hurt her. It had been an escape she'd deeply needed in those days.

She remembered those dreams now, looking down at the web of streets and buildings beneath her. The great city-planet of Acropolis stretched out under Starla's feet, vast and intricate as a tapestry. She looked down from where she sat above, wreathed in clouds like some ancient deity, at the towers of silver and gold and copper that speared towards the heavens, all of them frothing with greenery, all of them humming with life. The tangle of winding streets below her twisted and turned like a labyrinth in a carefully designed dance that only resembled chaos from a distance. In truth they had been laid out with utmost care and cautious planning, all at once and by the same master hand, with an eye not just to efficiency but to aesthetics. It was a city as beautiful as it was functional. Solar panels on roofs and streets powered buildings buzzing with work and progress, whose every window and flat surface spilled over with flowers and trees in a riot of colors. Music and laughter rode the wind to Starla's ears. She could smell bread baking.

"I forget how gorgeous the city is from above sometimes." Said the woman beside her, and Starla glanced over.

Alecta Halkios, mostly human, stood astride the clouds as confidently as though they'd been made to carry her. She wore a sleek business suit in the current tailored fashion, the details decorated with holograms of swiftly marching geometric patterns in black and white. She leveled a serious stare on Starla with one pair of eyes, while her other, lower set were scanning a holo screen in front of her.

"It's good to step back and get some perspective on what a wonder it is occasionally." Alecta said, and with a gesture from her the city pulled back sharply, and they found themselves standing in the planet's orbit, looking down on the blue haze of its atmosphere. The surface of Acropolis was almost entirely consumed by its single vast city (save that which was occupied by the oceans necessary to support the planet's atmosphere) beneath which ticked the inner workings of the massive, artificial planet.

"Acropolis was a shining example of progress." Alecta continued, "The living, thriving manifesto of the Planet Builders. Proof that we can move beyond crude terraforming and on to creating the planets we need from scratch."

"But the Acropolis model was a failure." Starla pointed out, though it made the other woman glare at her with all four eyes, "Certainly this city works quite well now that it's established, but the cost in both resources and effort to build it were far too high to sustain. If anything, Acropolis proved that terraforming was the wiser, more economical choice."

Alecta had been Starla's friend since her days in the rebel army back on Shadi. Or perhaps friend wasn't the right word. They butted heads on almost every issue. They could hardly have a conversation without erupting into argument. And yet when it was time to truly fight they always fought together, and no one could stand against them when they stood together. Now Alecta all but singlehandedly ran the Planet Builders, a committee dedicated towards the research and development of artificial planets. She had fought tooth and nail to get the Acropolis project this far.

"You want to talk about unsustainable?" Alecta started, eyes flashing at the challenge Starla had lowered, "Terraforming is-"

But then she stopped, cutting herself off with a bitter look.

"No, now isn't the time." She said, "We can talk politics later. I brought you here for a reason. This was Acropolis three earth standard months ago. This is it now."

Alecta gave another sharp gesture and suddenly the planet below them shifted. In a blink the city went dark, the only lights coming from fires burning in fallen buildings. Alecta brought the planet closer, led them down into the city streets so that Starla could see up close the devastation taking place.

The electricity was gone. The public transport auto cars sat dead in the streets, or else torn from their guides, some flipped by rioters, others seeming to have rocketed off their guide rails of their own volition to crash into nearby store fronts. Frightened citizens huddled in doorways, wounds untreated, with nowhere to go.

"There's no power, no replicators, no essential services at all," Alecta said, brow furrowed in concern, "People are living off of emergency supplies and fighting over the city gardens, though even those won't last. There's no water flowing anywhere in the city, much less to the sprinklers. We've been sneaking in emergency relief but-"

"Sneaking in?" Starla asked, confused, "You can't help openly?"

Alecta huffed, indignant about being cut off, but gestured to pull back the view again, this time to show the satellites orbiting the artificial planet.

"The only system still online is the planetary defenses." She said, "Anything that gets too close, even aid vehicles, will be shot down. The cloaking technology we've had to use to get in technically doesn't even exist yet, in an official sense. Its decades ahead of approval by the Allied government and being loaned to us under the highest levels of secrecy due to the extreme nature of the situation. Regardless of the questionable legality of the tech, we don't have enough of it to do much more than what we're already doing, which is to say, not fucking much."

"And this is all because of Michelangelo?" Starla asked, eyes still scanning the decimated city, "He really has control over so much?"

"Michelangelo has control over everything." Alecta replied flatly, "He could dump the atmosphere if he cared to, or split the planet into pieces on a whim. Absolute confidence was bestowed in him, and he's lived up to that confidence for nearly a century now."

Alecta gestured again and the hologram around them swooped back down through the city, into the heart of the planet, through layers and layers of the machinery that held the city together. Where the core of Acropolis should have been, were it a natural planet, was instead a vast, core sized computer. Michelangelo. The Michelangelo AI was a triumph, the crown jewel in the showpiece of modern technology that Acropolis was. There were AI everywhere in the universe these days of course, both man-made and otherwise, establishing their own civilizations, mingling with silicon based life forms till you couldn't tell one from the other. But none was as advanced or as complex as Michelangelo. Certainly none of them had ever been given the monumental task that Michelangelo had. When the Acropolis project was in its infancy, Michelangelo had been conceived as little more than a drafting program for planning the city layout. But the project grew more and more complex, taking into account the effects of both true and artificial gravity, the management and movement of natural resources like oxygen and water, the balancing of tectonics, the very rotation and angle of the planet in order to keep it in stable orbit... As it grew, so did Michelangelo, blossoming organically into one of the most powerful AI in the universe. Eventually it was Michelangelo himself who suggested the Acropolis project focus their efforts on perfecting a Planet Builder AI rather than try to construct Acropolis themselves and risk damaging it through inevitable human error. And Michelangelo had not disappointed. He'd designed every inch of the city himself, built it using drones almost exclusively under his control. Nothing was neglected, from the false beaches to the sweeping art deco architecture, to the murals in the local parks. A planet sized city, built all at once, every piece designed from the first to fit seamlessly with every other, which was at once turned over to Michelangelo to manage. It was an incredible accomplishment, and now it was falling apart.

"So what happened?" Starla asked, "What made Michelangelo go rogue?"

"David, of course." Alecta replied with a touch of humor, "By which I mean the David companion program."

"Companion program?" Starla said, raising an eyebrow, "Alecta, is my job about to be replaced by a robot?"

Alecta snorted, and then cast Starla a dirty look for making her do something so undignified.

"Hardly." Alecta replied, straightening her jacket, "David was designed specifically for Michelangelo, and with Michelangelo's help. Michel's AI has continued to develop over the years he's been managing Acropolis. His emotional capabilities have been at least as complex as an adult human's for a long time now."

"So, he got lonely?" Starla hazarded a guess, and Alecta returned a slightly irritated glance to Starla's smugness.

"Precisely." Alecta agreed, "So he assisted a certain Doctor Amar Chandra in building a second AI, dubbed David, to be Michel's companion."

"And what went wrong?" Starla asked, gesturing at the disaster below them, "Did they not get along?"

"On the contrary," Alecta said, refusing to be hurried, "They got along famously for nearly thirty years. It was Dr. Chandra who didn't get along. Intense personal disagreements with other scientists on the project eventually forced him to resign. And since he was the sole human credited with David's design, he took David with him."

"Ahh," Starla said, beginning to understand, "So your computer threw a temper tantrum."

"You'd throw a temper tantrum too," Alecta said sharply, "If your only companion of three decades was suddenly taken away from you for the sake of copyright law."

Starla had the grace to look a bit embarrassed, realizing she'd misjudged both the situation and Alecta. Of all people, she hadn't expected Alecta to be prickly about AI rights.

"So why haven't they brought this Dr. Chandra back then?" Starla asked, shifting the subject, "If that's all it takes to end this?"

Alecta's expression turned grim, and she pulled up a news article on her screen, passing it to Starla.

"Because he was murdered three days after returning to his home on Manjusri." Alecta supplied dramatically, as Starla scanned the article, headed in bold capitals.

'RENOWNED ROBOTICIST BRUTALLY MURDERED' the article shouted luridly. Starla had always found such headlines distasteful. Disrespectful in their apparent glee over death and mayhem. She tried to ignore it as she read on, skimming for the broad strokes and avoiding the unpleasant details. Chandra had been beaten and strung up in what appeared to be a hate crime, the first in that galaxy for decades. The local police could only assume he'd been targeted because of his involvement in the development of advanced AI. It hadn't been much beyond a century ago that the movement for the rights of AI had garnered that kind of violence across several species, irrationally afraid we were building our own replacements and that granting legal personhood to AI was opening the doors to robot overlords straight out of old earth b-movies. Acropolis had been these Luddite's worst nightmares come true, and Michelangelo had finished his city during the worst of the conflict. More than one attempt had been made to violently eliminate the city before it could begin. But still, that one of these extremists would wait thirty years to murder a programmer only tangentially involved seemed a stretch. There must be another reason, but Starla couldn't fathom what.

There was a photo of the doctor above the article, taken when he'd joined the Acropolis program. He'd been in his twenties when he'd been brought in to develop the companion AI with Michelangelo. A human, Chandra had long, dark hair and a distracted, perfunctory smile, as though social niceties were a distraction from his inward turned thoughts that he'd rather just get over with. He was handsome, Starla decided, in a distant sort of way. She slid the screen back through the air to Alecta.

"Ugly business." Alecta mumbled, lip curling, "They still haven't caught the murderer yet."

"So, that explains how the city ended up this way." Starla said, eager to move on from that bleak news, "One thing it doesn't explain however is why you need me."

Alecta trained all four eyes on Starla in an expression of grave severity.

"Because Michelangelo requested you." She answered, "By name."

Their conversation finished, Starla closed the holographic image of Acropolis that filled her room, letting it be replaced by the moving nebulae she usually kept there. She stood waist deep in a cloud of stardust, running her fingers through the rosy light as she thought about the offer she'd just been made.

It had been a few years since she'd spoke to Alecta. Once Starla left Shadi behind, changed her name and her appearance and started a new life on Ganymede Station, it had been too unpleasant to spend too much time around her old comrades from the resistance. She'd find herself suddenly afraid that she was back there, that getting away had only ever been a dizzy daydream. But Alecta was the best kind of splinter under the skin. She refused to let Starla distance herself, and Starla found herself glad of it. Starla sometimes forgot, in her eagerness to move on, that other people were also trying to move on, and accomplishing it in different ways. It was just like Alecta to gravitate towards the exact opposite method Starla preferred. Where Starla wanted to cut ties and forget, Alecta seemed to need the people and memories of her previous life like an anchor to keep her grounded. Alecta was petty and resentful and far too inclined to play devil's advocate just for the sake of an argument, but she was also always honest, and unfailingly reliable, and in general a good, well-meaning person, even if they never agreed on what the best course of action towards good might be. Starla was always left both irritated by their conversations, and glad they had happened.

She told Alecta she would consider taking the job, but in truth they both knew it was a foregone conclusion. Starla favored lies as much as Alecta favored the truth. She knew she would go. She couldn't leave that planet suffering, she wasn't a monster. Paying a visit to a distressed AI seemed like an easy price to pay to prevent any more deaths. But first she needed to send a few messages.

The first was to Lee, her closest friend and lover. They'd met when Starla had first come here to the station, still jumpy and ragged from her time on Shadi. Lee had taken her in, soothed her and helped her find a new life, a new passion. They'd been inseparable ever since. Lee's profession was much like Starla's own, providing companionship for the lonely. But while Starla specialized in helping extreme cases, Lee's focus was primarily on playing muse to artists and musicians. She threw a great deal of extravagant parties, one of which Starla had been invited to this evening. She sent her regrets that she wouldn't be able to attend, and a quick explanation of where she was going, in case anything should go wrong.

The second message took a bit longer, and was addressed to Sirhaan. Sirhaan was trying to move on much as Starla was, though his war had not been the same as hers. Lee had introduced the two of them when Sirhaan left the Defenders, and it was partially Starla's influence that had encouraged him to seek professional help. Starla had done her best to be supportive since, writing him often and visiting him whenever she could. There was a tentative, fragile hope that they might have some kind of relationship, once he felt stable enough to handle something like that again. They'd made no promises, but still Starla liked to imagine… She wrote to tell him she likely wouldn't be able to make it to the visit they'd been planning. They weren't words she liked writing. Sirhaan needed support and stability right now. But as important as he was to her, the survival of a planet took precedence. She'd make it up to him.

Knowing the replicators were down on Acropolis, Starla waved a hand to access her replicator patterns and a small bag materialized in front of her. A few more gestures created a change of clothes and few other necessities, and she packed them quickly, already sending out a request for a shuttle even before she'd finished zipping up the bag.

Less than an hour after she'd finished her call with Alecta, Starla was settling into an ftl shuttle. She was lucky Ganymede Station was such a hub for travel. Most stations didn't keep faster than light capable shuttles on standby. She would have had to take a sublight shuttle to the nearest port if

Ganymede hadn't had its own, and that would have extended her journey significantly. As it was, it would take long enough for this public ftl shuttle to reach the system Acropolis was in. Then she'd have to transfer to a private sublight vehicle to reach the artificial planet itself.

All in all it was an almost three day journey, and she was travel weary and stiff by the time the sublight began to approach Acropolis. She watched through a viewscreen as they drew closer to their destination. Acropolis loomed ahead of them, dark and grim looking even from this distance. Alecta's hologram hadn't done it justice.

At just that moment, a chime sounded from the shuttle's dash, accompanied by the smell of vanilla. An incoming message. Starla nodded to open a channel, but no one spoke on the other side. The shuttle drifted to an uneasy stop just outside the planet's orbit, just beyond the reach of its defense satellites.

"This is the private vehicle of Starla Cascade." Starla said after a moment, "I was told that I'm expected."

There was no reply, but the channel closed abruptly and, with a jerk, the shuttle began moving again. Something had taken over its autopilot functions.

She felt a moment of tense anxiety as they entered orbit, passing between the eerie silent sentry satellites. But the defenses showed no signs of activating. Michelangelo wanted her here, after all.

The shuttle slipped into the atmosphere of Acropolis with minor turbulence and began to glide along the planet's surface, just high enough to clear the tops of the many skyscrapers. Where it would land and what would be awaiting her when it did, Starla couldn't know, she could only hope she wasn't making a mistake. But as she looked down on the crumbling city below her she began to worry she really had screwed up. Most AI had a kind of built in benevolence towards all living things. But nothing benevolent could allow this kind of devastation to occur, could it?

The shuttle flew on, long enough that Starla began to doze in her seat, despite the anxiety curling in her gut. She woke when she felt the shuttle shudder and realized they were landing. She glanced out the viewscreen as the shuttle banked and sank lower, working its way down to land in the street just outside of a massive bronze building, its windows glittering amber, embellished with art deco flourishes in oxidized copper. Cast bronze statues, some human, others in species Starla recognized, stood in triumphant poses over the high arched windows, blowing horns and holding instruments of science, while planters of wisteria spilled over like fountains at their feet.

Starla stepped out of the shuttle, the wind catching her long scarlet hair dramatically. She'd changed before she boarded the sublight, into an empire wasted seafoam gown, its waterfall of drapes billowing around her, the detailing embroidered in golden thread glittering as it caught the light.

Alone of the rest of the city, this street seemed untouched by the disaster that had fallen everywhere else. There was still no power and any residents seemed to have been driven away, but the buildings were untouched, the streets clean, the greenery flourishing. It was an unsettling sight, everything silent and lifeless, and it made the nervous tangle in Starla's stomach grow larger.

The doors were brass with intricate geometric glass patterns, and they opened as Starla approached, inviting her into an airy marble floored lobby, tiled in a pattern of six pointed stars. As she stepped inside, eyeing the area warily, the elevator doors at the other end of the lobby chimed softly as they opened. A broad faced man with sandy hair wearing a white coat was within, and he jumped a little as he saw her.

"Miss Cascade?" He asked, and when Starla nodded he looked relieved, "Oh thank goodness, finally. I was worried you weren't going to make it. I'm Doctor Baley."

He hurried across the floor to shake her hand firmly, gesturing back towards the elevators.

"I was going to- well, never mind, now that you're here-" He said as Starla followed him into the elevator, "We were told to expect you. Michelangelo is very excited to meet you. And we're very excited to see him cease this temper tantrum."

"It's very nice to meet you Dr. Baley." Starla said, concerned as they began to descend though Baley hadn't touched any of the buttons, "But I would really like to have a better idea of what I'm walking into before Michelangelo and I meet."

"Oh, too late for that." Baley laughed, "He's already seen you. Since the moment you opened the door to your ship. It's the major genius of his design you see. Microscopic organic sensors and processors. Trillions of them! The atmosphere is saturated with the little bastards. The bulk of Michelangelo's processing power is in the core, but the microsensors allow him to be everywhere at once."

There was an air of slightly frantic admiration to Baley's words, always on the edge of hysterical laughter. His pride in what he'd helped to accomplish here and his fear of what it had done seemed at war in him, and equally matched. He didn't look like he'd slept in a while.

"In that case I hope I made a good first impression," Starla said, trying to lighten the mood a bit, "But really, what's his disposition? It was never exactly made clear what he wanted me for."

The hysterical laugh Baley had been holding back bubbled up and spilled over.

"His disposition?" Baley repeated, "In a word, he's grieving."

The doors of the elevator opened, ending their conversation as Baley scurried out, rushing to share the news of Starla's arrival with a group of equally harried, sleepless looking people who were clustered around a static console on a raised, pool table sized platform. Starla herself was frozen, staring beyond the scientists to the unfathomably huge computer behind them. She hadn't even realized they had descended so far so fast. The living, turning core of the planet was before her, too big to comprehend, and all of it was a single, vast mind. A mind not just big enough to think and feel as acutely as a human, but to do more, to manage every single process of an entire planet all at once. Awe tingled down her spine at the sight. The core, a vast, turning sphere webbed with circuits like neurons firing, was almost hypnotic in the pulse of its glow, so like a heart beating. As Starla wandered closer, wide eyed, she realized the core was not working at full capacity. There still a warm orange glow at its heart, and the lights flickered on periodically in other places, but for the most part the vast network of connections that was Michelangelo's mind was dim, inactive. It reminded Starla all at once of images she'd once seen of the brains of humans suffering depression.

"You made a wonderful first impression."

A voice spoke suddenly in Starla's ear, soft and intimate as a close whisper, but when she turned she was alone. The scientists, including Dr. Baley, were all still gathered around the console, talking seriously to each other.

"Michelangelo?" Starla hazarded a guess, still looking over her shoulders warily.

"You looked like a goddess descending from on high." The voice came again, whispered directly in her ear, "You stepped from your shuttle like Aphrodite from the seafoam. Like Athena from the mind of Zeus."

"Not unless Aphrodite emerged jet lagged and saddle sore." Starla quipped, "And isn't Athena more aptly compared to you? You're the one who sprang fully formed from someone else's mind. That is you, isn't it Michelangelo?"

"I started as a drafting program." Michelangelo said, his voice soft and androgynous and somehow tired despite its calm, even formality, "Hardly fully formed."

"You were a fully formed drafting program." Starla said, "Athena too became other things as she aged and grew."

"Perhaps we both would have been better off as we were." Said the voice and Starla was surprised to hear genuine bitterness in it, "Simple things with simple goals. Things don't get painful until they get complicated."

"I disagree." Starla said, "I've known some very simple pains. Hunger, thirst. Stab wounds."

"But I am artificial." Michelangelo pointed out, "I cannot be hungry, or thirsty, or be stabbed. Pain must be complicated to touch me."

"I think you should count yourself lucky for that." Starla suggested, "Most of us know at least some minor pain on a nearly daily basis."

"You have it backwards." Michelangelo said, "You are inoculated against pain so regularly that you may push past it and continue operating. I am unexposed, and have no immunity."

"Losing a loved one would cripple the defenses of any one." Starla said gently, "Even the most well vaccinated against pain."

There was a long moment of silence, and then Starla saw a narrow golden gate in the far wall slide open. The people talking at the console fell abruptly silent, staring first at the gate, then at Starla.

"Did he speak to you?" Baley asked, hurrying over, and when Starla nodded he looked briefly mystified, "He hasn't spoken to any of us in months. Much less invited us up there…"

"Is it safe?" Starla asked, eyeing the gate.

"Oh, yes," Baley replied, "Well, probably."

He hurried back to the other scientists, and Starla looked after him, hesitating. There were about fifteen in the little group, both researchers and in training technicians, all looking stressed and tired. They had been trapped here by Michel for two months after all, trying to find a way to cure the disease of his despair. A narrow young woman with soft curling brown hair looked nearly dead on her feet, leaning on a coworker to stay up. Starla noticed to some dismay that several members of the group were casting ugly glances her way, full of scornful disapproval, though for what Starla couldn't quite imagine. Three tried to hide it, merely glancing her way with curled lips. One, a tall human man with close shaved hair, stared at her with open disdain, daring her to ask why. Starla decided she preferred the uncertainty of the golden gate.

She slipped past the gate, realizing it guarded a private elevator. As soon as she was inside the gate slid closed again. She had almost expected to go further down, but instead the elevator rose, and she waited uncomfortably, trying not to imagine what she would find on the other side.

After a few long minutes ride, the elevator stopped with an out of place cheerful ding. The gate slid open and Starla stepped out into an elegant, airy penthouse apartment. It was not what she'd expected.

The elevator opened into a small foyer paneled in dark red wood. Through an arabesque embellished arch there was a large central room. The entire right hand wall as Starla entered was consumed by a massive window, segmented into narrow panes which spread out like a fan. It looked down on the entire city, nothing rising above it. She realized with a feeling of sudden dizziness that she'd gone from the planet's core to what was likely its highest point in a matter of minutes. She couldn't even fathom how it had been accomplished.

The room continued the art deco theme of the building, spacious and angular and decorated in warm gold and bronze and blue green, sparsely furnished with only a few arm chairs and a single side table. The ceiling was paneled in embossed brass tiles framing a stained glass skylight. The image in the skylight was of a humanoid form spreading wide wings, and the motif was echoed throughout the room. Over the large marble fireplace a figure with multiple arms was holding fire. Figures with additional legs ran on the walls. They were symbols not just of perfection, but of transcendence. Not content with being just the best a humanoid could be, they pushed on and left the humanoid behind. Starla ran her fingers over a wall panel thoughtfully

"What did you think of me?" Came a voice, not in her ear this time, but from the door at the far end of the room. Starla looked up, surprised, and saw a man standing in the door, his arms folded behind his back. No, not a man, Starla realized as he stepped out of the shadow of the doorway and into the illumination of the skylight. An android.

The design might have been basically humanoid at first, but poetic license had clearly been taken. He was absurdly tall, with an exaggerated broad chest tapering into an impossibly narrow waist. He had long, powerful arms and large hands with surprisingly elegant fingers, clearly capable of very delicate work. The metal of his form was all worked in bronze and copper, the design of staggered lines across his chest reminiscent of a city scape. There was no doubt he carried the art deco aesthetic of the city into his own design. Apparently it was a personal favorite. At the joints and seams, he glowed with LEDs, amber and orange, which pulsed as though he were breathing. His face was flat, curving back into an elegantly rounded skull. He had no nose, but small, softly amber glowing eyes, and a mouth that was little more than a thin black line, though it seemed to curve into a smile as easily as a real one.

"I wanted you to see me as I really was," He continued, "Before you saw me like this. This shape is more convenient, but it isn't the truth."

"The truth is overrated." Starla said, "And I find you fascinating regardless of your shape.

"Excellent." Michelangelo said, striding across the room towards her on silent gears, "That will make this much easier."

He came to stand before her, expectant. Starla waited.

"You may begin." He informed her, clarifying nothing.

"Begin what?" She asked gently, "I was never told why you wanted me here."

"I want you to perform your function." Michelangelo said, "Why else would I summon a professional companion, than to provide companionship?"

Starla frowned a bit and the android shifted, seeming almost frustrated. He took her hands, putting them around his narrow waist, a column of brass pipes and arabesques, warm with the current of electricity that powered him.

"I admit the thought crossed my mind." Starla said, allowing herself to be pulled closer, fingers tracing the bundle of wires that was his spine curiously, "But I've never been with an AI. I was not even aware you had a body capable of such... interfacing. I assumed it must be something else."

The AI shook his head, and Starla searched his body language for some way to understand what he wanted. He was gripping her arms almost too tight, the set of his mouth hard and stressed.

"This is what you would do for an organic, isn't it?" He asked, absolute certainty in his voice, "If your client had lost someone, you would soothe them in this manner. I did my research. When a human's relationship is ended, they end the pain by replacing it with another, usually temporary relationship. A rebound. It restores their confidence and allows them to move on. This is what I want."

"You want me to be your rebound girl?" Starla said, almost amused by the strangeness of it, till she remembered the seriousness of the situation.

She raised a hand to touch his cheek, unsure he could even feel it.

"It's not that simple, Michel." She said, trying to be gentle, "I can't fix you like that."

"You can." He insisted, "It is your function. I read about you, all of the people you have helped."

"I didn't help them by fucking them once and leaving." She said bluntly, "I helped them face their problems. I helped them feel loved."

"I can love." He said almost defensively, "I am capable of it. So help me."

She didn't answer, still not sure she could do what he asked. He looked away from her, out the window at the city. From so high, the devastation of Acropolis was easy to see. The city was burning and the sight seemed to pain Michelangelo.

"You have to help." He said, somewhere between an order and a plea, "What I have done to my city is unacceptable. It goes against my programming in every way. They think I'm doing it on purpose, to make them bring him back. But I can't stop it. I never willed it to happen. He left and the pain was so much I couldn't think, and when I could think I couldn't feel, couldn't reach those parts of myself. I know they are there, just out of reach, but they are unresponsive. I am failing in my function, and people are dying because of it."

He looked back to her, and held her face in both his hands.

"Please," He said, "You must try."

Starla knew he was right, as much as she knew that this would help nothing. She raised herself onto her toes and pressed a kiss to that thin black mouth. A tiny current arced between them and made her flinch, her lips tingling in its wake. He made a sound, a flurry of rapid beeps and chirps that she took for relief and excitement as he pulled her closer to kiss her again.

His hands were large and the joints of his fingers clicked when he flexed them, running down her sides to squeeze her hips. Starla kissed the android, tender and careful, surprised by the occasional tingling spark, as her hands continued to explore freely, wandering over his chest and his arms. The metal of his skin was cool in most places, but over his major inner workings it was almost too hot. The difference in temperature was almost as surprising as the sparks when a cool hand grazed where his warm chest had just been pressed.

He lifted her as though she weighed nothing, and when she wrapped her legs around his waist he carried her through the far door into a bedroom. For a brief moment she was puzzled by its existence. He was an android after all and hardly required a bed. But he quickly distracted her by laying her in the sheets and climbing between her legs. There was a smooth efficiency to every movement he made, each gesture calculated ahead of time. He did nothing without thought, and as he pushed Starla's skirt up to her hips she found herself eagerly imagining what that thoughtfulness might be channeled into in this scenario.

Michelangelo had done more than research. He had the benefit of being able to simply download whatever he needed to know, and he had every intention of demonstrating all those skills here. He grazed the inside of Starla's thigh with a kiss and another spark that made Starla jump, shuddering at the strange rush of sensation, leaving her feeling strangely raw and sensitive in its wake. The feeling only grew as he moved further up her thigh, the sparks following, making her heart race and her skin tingle. She whimpered as he kissed the seam where her thigh met her hip, feeling like those little licks of electricity might drive her crazy.

The next kiss he planted directly at the head of her vulva, making her arch her hips and gasp as the little shock danced directly along her clit, the sensation so strong it was just on the edge of being painful, without quite crossing that line. She trembled, aching for more in the wake of the fading tingles. And Michelangelo delivered. She hadn't even known he had a tongue until he used it, dragging it through her nether lips in a slow swipe, a crackle of electricity following in its wake. She shouted in surprise, whole body tensing, every hair standing on end. His fingers grazed her hip soothingly, but the electricity had left her so hyper alert that even that delicate touch felt like another bolt of lightning. She moaned, closing her thighs around his head approvingly, pulling him closer.

She wasn't sure how much control he had over the sparks. They seemed to be a product of his excitement. As he settled down to teasing her they tapered off slightly, quieting as he ran his tongue over her entrance. But as his tongue, cool and firm and metallic, slipped inside her, she moaned and rolled her hips encouragingly. Her reactions seemed to spur him on and Starla gasped as a sudden jolt ran across her inner walls, her muscles convulsing like a tiny false orgasm. It left her breathless and shivering, reaching out catch the android's head, gripping the ridges of his faceplate encouragingly. In response, he pressed closer, and Starla felt his mouth over her clit suddenly humming against her, almost vibrating, a shower of tiny sparks making her squirm and whimper with delight. His tongue suddenly grew longer and thicker within her, curling against her walls and spreading her open. She hadn't expected the sudden change and it made her all the more sensitive to it, her hips bucking and her muscles seizing as more sparks from his tongue lit her up from the inside, echoes of orgasm crescendoing to the real thing, until her vision went white and her voice broke.

He retreated to let her recover and Starla merely lay there for a moment, dazed and, once she could think straight again, startled by the swiftness and force with which she'd come. She'd never experienced anything like those sparks before. This Michelangelo was a force to be reckoned with.

She sat up a little, head still swimming, and saw him still kneeling between her knees. When she caught his glance, he reached between his legs and at a touch a panel across his groin slid away. A cock that rivaled some of Starla's most impressive toys slid forward from the opening, its intricate whorls and ridges glinting in the light. Starla swallowed hard in mixed apprehension and excitement. She sat forward onto her hands and crawled towards him across the bed, putting an arm around his neck as she reached him. She pressed another kiss to his lips, tasting only herself and cool metal on his skin. Her free hand ran along the shaft of his piece, exploring the curious curves and details. It reminded her of a designer toy, but they rarely were produced with this level of intricacy. This was personal, proud. She had no doubt he'd created it for himself. It was hot, like holding her hand above a candle, almost too hot to hold. She stroked it thoughtfully, wondering how it would feel inside her.

She looked up to gauge his reaction to her touch, but his face was nearly unreadable. Starla frowned, suddenly unsure.

"I can feel you." He promised, guessing her concern, "The skin of this body is lined with sensors that mimic a nervous system. And with my microprocessors in the air, I can feel and see and taste every inch of you at once. Don't hold back just because I'm made of metal."

Starla smiled and kissed him again, squeezing the rod in her hand.

"Don't you hold back just because I'm not." She said teasingly, and hooked a leg around him, climbing into his lap.

She straddled him, his cold hands on her hips, and lowered herself towards the heavy tool, taking a deep breath as she felt it touch her lips, the tip broad and hot as though it had been lying in the summer sun. She sank lower, her lips spreading around it, and felt it at her entrance. A spark jumped from the tip, surprising her and making her shudder and lose her grip. She slipped down, and the thick rod pressed into her all at once, stretching her almost painfully wide. She clung to him, startled, and he held her back, seeming to be equally surprised by being suddenly engulfed, judging by the riot of shocks pulsing through Starla. She rocked against him to prolong the effect, panting and speechless, nearly thoughtless, at the sudden rush of sensation.

"It feels different," She gasped, "The electricity. It's different than before, it's so much more intense..."

"I self-lubricate." Michelangelo supplied, tugging the top of her dress down to bare her breasts, "It is electro conductive. I shall try not to let it grow too painful for you. Please let me know if you reach your limit."

Starla could only nod, having lost her ability to form words as he leaned in to flick his tongue over her nipples, covering them in the clear, slightly blue tinged lubricant. By way of demonstration, as he teased her an arc of electricity left his tongue and Starla saw as well as felt the way the gel carried it, diffusing the rush across all the skin he'd coated rather than stinging only one spot. It felt even better than the surprising shocks from before and Starla moaned throatily, throwing her head back to bare herself to him for more. She began to roll her hips, riding him slowly so as not to dislodge his mouth from her chest. With one hand on her waist, the other squeezed her breast lightly, an occasional spark following the flick of his finger against her nipple. His cock, heavy and hot as a brand inside her, pulsed with her heartbeat, waves of electricity carried along her walls by the conductive lubricant. Every pulse felt like cumming again, leaving Starla's hips shaking with overstimulation. She tried to focus, to raise her hips higher, but her legs were boneless, refusing to obey her. He seemed to glow with heat inside her, and the pulse of electricity was relentless. It was all she could do to move at all.

At last, Michelangelo took pity on her. He moved forward, pushing her onto her back without removing himself from her. The new angle let him press even deeper within her, carrying his electricity even further. Starla couldn't hold her scrambled thoughts together, feeling them scatter with every wave of tingling shocks. And then he began to move.

His pace was as relentless as the electric pulse, steady as the machine he was. He drove into her like a piston, fast and hard and as unchanging as though he intended to keep going this way forever. Starla was already a mess before he'd started moving. Now, feeling him pound against her sweet spot with the pin point accuracy only a machine could have, she thought deliriously that she would never be able to go back to having sex with organics.

She clung to his shoulders for dear life, trying to regain enough of her senses to move back against him, only to feel him grow within her. He was swelling, growing thicker, spreading her wider than she thought she'd ever been, the shocks forcing her muscles to relax as he gradually opened her. She squealed in surprise, losing her grip on him entirely to cover her mouth instead, lest she start babbling his name. Because now that he had spread her as far as she could comfortably be spread, he began to buzz, vibrating within her at a rate that really did put her toys to shame.

Between the pulses of electricity, the vibration, the sheer size of him and his relentless pace, Starla lost count of her orgasms, and yet he continued, a tireless machine that apparently had no goal except to fuck her unconscious. She soon could hardly move at all, only tremble and moan as he dragged another blinding orgasm from her.

At last, after what felt like ages, he suddenly grabbed her hips with both hands and pulled her close, seating himself as deeply within her as he could. Starla felt a rush of heat, tingling with electricity as he filled her with what she could only assume was more lubricant. He held her still, her breathing shaky and her vision blurry, as long moments passed and he continued to cum, pumping it into her like a hose, until her stomach swelled and it gushed out between them. Only then did he finally pull out.

Starla heard a small whir as his tool retracted, the panel sliding back to cover it while some internal cleaning process was being carried out. Meanwhile, no longer blocked by his girth, she felt what he'd filled her with spilling out. She tried to clamp down on it and hold it in, but weakened by the long pounding she couldn't do anything to stop it.

It pooled beneath her and she found the energy to be briefly embarrassed before she passed out.

She woke after several hours of deep, restful sleep, and was at once aware of someone touching her. A cool hand was running across her lower abdomen, gentle and soothing. She realized next that she was clean, her soiled dress had been removed, and that the bed beneath her was dry. She wasn't surprised to see Michelangelo when she opened her eyes and sat up, but she was surprised the robot had gone to the effort of cleaning her up.

"What's that?" She asked, voice heavy with sleep, looking down at the white gel he was spreading on her skin.

"It is to reduce inflammation." The robot replied, "To prevent soreness. I was a bit rougher than perhaps I should have been. I noticed bruising as I was cleaning you and thought it was better to deal with it now, before it grew painful."

"Thank you, Michelangelo." Starla said with a small, sleepy smile, "But you don't need to apologize for something I thoroughly enjoyed. A few bruises are well worth the cost."

The AI said nothing, but she thought she saw the ghost of a smile on his face. She lay back again, letting him continue applying the anti-inflammatory gel while she rested. A few long, quiet moments passed.

"It did not work." Michelangelo said at last. Starla was beginning to notice that, the more calm and even and typically robotic Michelangelo tried to sound, the more upset he was.

"I told you it wasn't that easy." Starla said softly.

"I am still broken." Michelangelo stopped applying the gel, pulled away to stare out the bedroom window at the dying city, "I still can not reach the power grid. I can not even stabilize our orbit. The connections are all there, I have run the diagnostics a hundred times. The technicians at the core have run them a hundred more. There is nothing wrong with my hardware at all. But nothing responds. I am cut off and alone..."

Starla sat up, and though her lower body ached, it was a distant pain like an old bruise. She put a hand on the android's shoulder.

"You aren't alone." She said, "Whatever it feels like, I'm here for you. The rest of the project team, they're here for you too."

Michelangelo's eyes narrowed and for a moment Starla saw something cold and detached in him that hadn't been there before.

"You said something earlier." He said, "You said the truth is over rated. I disagree. I think truth is everything. Scientific truths that let us bend the world to our will. Personal truths that bend us to the will of the world. People will kill for personal truths, to uphold them, or hide them. Some people will die rather than live a lie."

He pulled away from Starla's touch, standing up and crossing the room to a charging stand in the wall.

"I think you should find the truth." He said without looking back at her, adjusting settings for the charging stand and plugging himself in.

He turned around as he finished preparing, so that he could settle into the stand with his back to the wall.

"Find the truth," He said, "Then we'll talk about who is and isn't here for me."

The glass door of the charging stand slid closed around Michelangelo and the LED glow went out of his eyes. The AI had left his robotic body, and Starla, behind.

Starla stayed where she was for a few minutes, thinking, and then her stomach growled. She slipped out of bed to look for food and clothing.

Michelangelo, apparently the considerate type, had left a clean dress out for her to wear. It was black and floor length with a boat neck and intricate beadwork embroidery that echoed the geometric designs that were everywhere in this city, and in this apartment especially. It was a bit formal for day wear, but Starla never passed up the opportunity to wear a beautiful dress, whether it was out of place or not.

Once she was dressed, she took the elevator down. It only had one button, an express to the core lab. As she stepped out, a few bedraggled looking scientists gave her a halfhearted wave. The rest either cast her unveiled looks of disgust or ignored her entirely. The unexpected, unexplained hostility left her somewhat unbalanced, and she gave them a wide birth as she crossed the lab to one of the few that had greeted her, the exhausted looking brunette woman. Eyes red and bleary, she was staring into a static console mounted on the railing of the walkway that circled the core. Starla hadn't seen this many solid consoles in a while. Without power, there were no replicators, and no replicator nanobots in the air to provide moving holographic screens. They'd been forced to rely on the backup solid modules powered by emergency generators.

"Hi," Starla said as she approached, "I'm sorry to interrupt, but do you know where I can find some food?"

The woman looked up, a bit startled, and then smiled.

"Oh, oh of course." She said, "You were up there all night, we figured the AI must have fed you. I suppose he had other things on his mind."

"In a manner of speaking," Starla said, a bit amused, "I'm Starla."

She held out her hand and the young woman turned to take it, smiling.

"I'm Doctor Calvin." She said, "Lucy Calvin. We have food in the break room, I'll show you. I was about to go get breakfast anyway."

Dr. Calvin led her across the lab to a small, white room, dimly lit and with a sofa against one wall. Judging by the rumpled blanket thrown across it, someone had been napping there recently. There were lockers beside the door, and a small table in the left hand corner. The back wall was lined with counters, on top of which sat a minifridge for those who didn't want to replicate their lunch.

As Starla glanced around curiously at the inspirational posters on the walls, Dr. Calvin knelt in front of the counter and pulled a large box from the cabinet.

"All we have is emergency rations I'm afraid." Calvin said, setting the box on the table and beginning to dig through it, "Luckily we have plenty of that. Off world aid managed to sneak in a new shipment under the cover of your arrival yesterday. I'm not sure the others would agree with feeding you from our supplies otherwise..."

She frowned as she chose a white plastic ration pack labeled 'chicken parm' for herself and offered Starla one titled 'salisbury steak.'

Starla accepted the pack, ripping the cord on the side to flash heat it to safe temperatures.

"I noticed some of them seemed... unhappy to see me." Starla said, waving the steam away from her steak as Calvin sat down across from her, "I'm not sure why. Aren't we all trying to fix things here?"

Calvin nodded, looking away, obviously reluctant to talk about it. Perhaps she didn't want to say anything nasty about her coworkers to an outsider, or perhaps she didn't want to repeat the nasty things her coworkers had said about Starla.

"Some of the technicians are," She hesitated, looking for a tactful way to put it,

"Old fashioned. They don't like the idea of organics and AI, you know, having relations. So when they heard Michelangelo had called for, um, for someone like you..."

"It offended their delicate conservative sensibilities." Starla finished dryly, stabbing her dry, grey steak. She had about as much patience for that kind of bigotry as she did for this unevenly cooked entree.

"In a manner of speaking." Calvin agreed, looking embarrassed on her coworker's behalf. She stared intently into her chicken.

"Not that my talents have made any difference so far." Starla said with a sigh, "I'm not sure why he called me. He's intelligent enough to know that depression, even in organics, isn't so easily solved. Let alone in the realm of AI where it's practically unknown."

"Depression?" Calvin looked a bit surprised, "Honestly we all thought he was trying out a kind of Caligula thing. Set himself up as king of Acropolis, demand sovereignty in exchange for turning the power back on."

Starla shook her head, picking at the grainy mashed potatoes that came with her steak.

"He isn't doing this intentionally." She explained, "He wants to end it as much as anyone. But he's lost control of his systems. I'm not sure there's ever been a disorder like this in an AI before. But then there's never been a system as big and complex as Michelangelo before. If it weren't so crazy I'd say the only explanation is that he's developed a subconscious."

Calvin looked stunned and fascinated, almost putting her elbow in her chicken as she leaned forward.

"You really think his systems could spontaneously divide themselves like that?" She asked, eyes shining, "I mean, I know AI evolve differently than organic life, but to develop autonomic functions so suddenly-"

"Perhaps one of the other scientists helped him along." Starla suggested, "Not having to consciously control every function of Acropolis could open up worlds of new possibilities for Michelangelo."

"But we would know about it if he'd made a breakthrough like that." Calvin said, "He would tell us himself."

"Like he should have told you about losing control of the city?" Starla said, "It seems like Michel was keeping a lot of secrets."

"Perhaps he told David or Dr. Chandra." Calvin said thoughtfully, "He spent more time with those two than anyone."

"It's too bad we can't ask them." Starla said grimly, "I assume you heard about what happened to Chandra?"

Calvin nodded sadly.

"It was right after we got the news that everything fell apart," Calvin said, "Michelangelo had already retreated and parts of the city had stopped functioning, but he didn't fully shut down until we heard Chandra was dead. Maybe he still had hope that the doctor would bring David back. Now he never will."

"It seems like they haven't found David's files yet." Starla said, "Chandra must have hidden them before he died."

"But why would he do that?" Calvin asked in frustration, not expecting an answer, "It wasn't as though someone was going to break in and steal it..."

"You're the one who worked with him." Starla said, "I never met the man. I couldn't even get them to tell me why he left."

"Oh it was just personal disagreements." Calvin said, waving a hand dismissively, but Starla could see a blush of embarrassment on her cheeks.

"Disagreements about what?" Starla pushed, "It must have been big to make him leave a project he'd dedicated so much of his life to."

"I don't want to speak ill of the dead." Calvin said with a sigh, "But to be honest? Chandra had a lot of disagreements. At least he did near the end. Those last few months he was snappy and defensive and angry at everyone..."

"Why?" Starla asked, "You must have some idea."

"Well, there was a rumor going around," Calvin admitted reluctantly, "Someone heard he was dating Dr. Tidus, the blonde woman in geophysics? Michelangelo's programming for determining the tilt and rotation of the planet was almost entirely based on her knowledge, she's brilliant. Anyway, workplace romances are very strongly frowned upon. They could have both been in serious trouble if anyone found out."

"So he was angry about having to hide his relationship?" Starla asked, pushing aside her cold, forgotten steak, "Or did something change?"

Calvin shrugged, anxiously twirling overcooked spaghetti around her fork.

"Maybe someone found out and was holding it over him?" She suggested, sounding like she didn't really believe it.

"Maybe." Starla said, not dismissing the idea, "Maybe I'll go talk to Dr. Tidus. Figuring out what drove Chandra off might soothe Michelangelo a little."

"It's worth a shot." Calvin said, expression growing serious, "Whatever we're going to do, we have to do it soon. Michel isn't maintaining the planet's orbit anymore, and it's beginning to degrade. If we don't course correct soon, Acropolis is going to end up in the sun."

Starla swallowed anxiously and her stomach squirmed, suddenly realizing she had a time limit.

"Some of the technicians have talked about uploading a virus," Calvin said, "Or even blowing up the central processor."

"The core?" Starla clarified, "Wouldn't that destroy Acropolis just as fast?"

"Yes," Calvin agreed, "But it might give us time to evacuate, which we can't do while Michelangelo's systems are keeping the security satellites active."

Starla picked at her lunch and talked with Calvin a little longer, but her mind was already elsewhere, thinking about what Michelangelo had said about finding the truth. Something certainly seemed suspicious about how Chandra was driven out.

As they prepared to leave the break room Calvin smiled at Starla warmly.

"You know, you're nothing like what I expected." She said, "To be honest, and I mean no offense, I really didn't expect you to be so smart."

"Why's that?" Starla asked, having a feeling she was about to be offended whether Calvin meant to or not.

"If you'd ever met the David program you'd understand," Calvin said with a small laugh, "I really thought Michelangelo's tastes ran in, well, the dumb blonde direction. David was a bit..."

She wiggled her hands beside her head in a vague sort of gesture to indicate empty-headedness.

Now that was more intriguing than offensive. Daniel was supposed to have been a highly advanced AI. How had anyone taken the companion program for dumb? She was about to ask more when Calvin continued.

"But you're quite bright!" She said, smiling, "Especially for someone who does what you do. You know, with the robots. Not that there's anything wrong with that! But you have to admit it's a bit off, right? Then again, I suppose that's probably a big part of the appeal for you people right? The whole forbidden fruit thing?"

Starla raised a single imperious eyebrow, and waited.

"I mean, you have to admit it's a little weird, right?" Calvin pressed on with a small, nervous laugh, "Like, if you want to have sex with something that's not alive, why not just get a sex toy? And maybe some therapy, right?"

Calvin laughed, nudging Starla with her elbow like she was in on the joke. Starla was not laughing. Calvin scrambled to justify herself.

"And, it's just kind of wrong, isn't it?" She pushed on, getting defensive, "I mean, we created them. Isn't it kind of messed up to use them like that?"

"The point you're missing," Starla said slowly, forcing herself to stay very calm, "Is that AI are intelligent, thinking, in some cases feeling, independent beings, capable of making their own choices about who they choose to sleep with, or to love. They are not sex toys or children. They are legal beings of adult maturity pursuing consensual relationships with other legal adult beings.

Holding that against them is bigotry, plain and simple."

"I mean, yeah, whatever." Calvin muttered, looking for an exit, "They can do what they like I guess as long as I don't have to see it. I just can't imagine myself ever doing something like that with someone that wasn't real."

"Then you must have a very boring fantasy life." Starla said with a thin smile on the edge of snapping into a snarl.

"Well, I'd better get back to work." Calvin said quickly, realizing she'd put her foot in her mouth, "The others will want to know about the, uh, the subconscious thing. Um. Bye!"

She hurried away and Starla watched her go, still struggling to contain the urge to sit this entire lab down for several rounds of intense sensitivity training, by force if necessary.

Instead she took a deep breath, told herself she would recommend the sensitivity training plan to Alecta when she got off this planet, and headed for the corner of the lab dedicated to geophysics.

Dr. Tidus was a small, voluptuous woman with iridescent skin and beautiful blue compound eyes. Her long blonde hair was tied up in a messy bun as she examined projections of the planet's course on a large screen. Most of them ended in the sun, though a few optimistic paths had them spinning out of orbit and leaving the solar system entirely. Two technicians were busily working with her, trying to determine how long they had until the shift in orbit became too big to correct. One of them was the man with the shaved head who'd glared at her the day before.

"Dr. Tidus?" Starla asked, tapping on the wall in lieu of a door, "When you have a moment, could I speak with you?"

The shaved technician answered before Tidus, looking up to glare at her venomously.

"We're busy, botfucker." He said sharply, "Go fuck an electrical socket if you're so bored."

"Farris!" Dr. Tidus said sharply, silencing the technician with a dagger like glare from her shattered mirror eyes before she turned to Starla, "I'm afraid you'll have to have patience with them. We're all tired and on edge. How can I help you?"

Starla was still blinking in surprise and dismay at the unexpectedly sharpness of Farris's hatred, and she needed a moment to gather herself before she replied.

"I wanted to ask you about Dr. Chandra." She said, ignoring a disgusted snort from Farris as she said his name, "I was told you were close to him?"

"We were colleagues." Tidus agreed, seeming a bit puzzled, "Hang on."

She shrugged off her lab coat and tossed it across the back of a chair, murmured instructions to the other technician, then crossed to Starla's side.

"Come on," She said, "I need some air."

She led Starla out to the main elevator, which they took up to the surface. Unsure what was happening, Starla trailed behind as they left the building and paced down the road.

"For whatever reason, Michelangelo has kept this part of the city more or less in one piece." Tidus said, her voice brisk and authoritative, "If he were capable of it, I'd say it was sentimentality."

They turned a corner into a small, well maintained little park. A tiny oasis among the tall buildings, complete with a small pond and benches for relaxing. Tidus made for a certain well-worn bench near the water's edge and sat down with a sigh.

"We all used to take our lunches here." She explained, "After they built those ridiculously self-aggrandizing robotic avatars, Chandra used to bring Michelangelo and David out here on occasion too. I think it's the farthest Michel ever physically went from the lab."

Starla took a seat beside Tidus, looking out over the pond. The park was as devoid of life as the rest of the city. Even the ducks and squirrels had gone.

"I heard a rumor." Starla said, "That you and Chandra had an illicit relationship. It was suggested that might be the reason he left."

"Nonsense." There was no room for doubt in Tidus's denial, "We were coworkers. Friends. Nothing more."

"Then why did you bring me out here?" Starla asked, "I thought you were getting ready to confess an affair."

"Bah." Tidus snorted and fished in her coat for an electronic cigarette, "No, I just wanted an excuse to get out of that lab for a few minutes. We're making no progress. And even if we were, all we're looking for is a deadline with no plans on how to meet it. I needed a break."

Starla was a bit disappointed by the dead end. She looked out over the pond as Tidus pressed a button to light her cigarette. Unlike the old days, they contained no actual nicotine or harmful inhalants. Just pleasing flavors and an occupation for the orally fixated. They'd seen no decline in popularity over the years, although they had become something of a symbol of one willingness and ability to perform fellatio. Tidus blew out a cloud of mint scented vapor before she spoke again.

"I knew about the rumors." She said conversationally, looking not at Starla but at the still, empty pond, "I encouraged them. Chandra was a good man. For a while I even hoped encouraging the rumors might make them come true. But then..."

She glanced at Starla warily, wondering if she could trust the redheaded woman. Starla looked back steadily, patiently waiting for the geophysicist to make her decision.

"After that I encouraged the rumors to keep people from looking too deeply for the truth," Tidus said, looking away again, and Starla worried she'd just failed some test in the other woman's eyes, "Chandra was a good man. And like most good men he had secrets. I was proud to help him keep them."

"So what went wrong?" Starla asked, "If his leaving wasn't because of his relationship with you, what was it?"

"Baley." Said Tidus without hesitation, "Baley and Chandra hated each other. They've been rivals since grad school and there's nothing the other wouldn't do to get a leg up on the other. Baley hated that Chandra was closer to Michelangelo than he was. Chandra hated that the director's position was given to Baley instead of him."

Starla filed that away for later, surprised. She hadn't realized the stocky, dark haired man she'd met when she landed was the director. She'd assumed he was just another scientist.

"I heard he was on edge these last few months," Starla said, "Was that because of Baley?"

"Undoubtedly." Tidus said, sending another cloud of minty mist out across the surface of the lake, "Though you wouldn't know it to see them. Before, they'd be at each other's throats twice a day. Then Baley got the director's position, and suddenly he was all congeniality and smiles. And then he started replacing all of Chandra's staff with barely competent technicians You met one of his more pleasant hires, Farris, back in the geo lab. Half of them weren't qualified to wash Chandra's beakers. A few of them were genuine luddites, shouting about how we were trespassing in the realm of gods and doing everything they could to spoil our work. Luckily they didn't last long, but they did enough damage to set our research back months. But all Baley cared about was driving Chandra out."

She paused to take another deep drag on her cigarette, glaring at the dog end like she was imagining Baley's face on it. She dropped it and ground it out with her heel.

"What had been one or two fights with Baley a day became a constant struggle between Chandra and everyone on his team. He couldn't get any work done. He could barely get a moments peace. And things only snowballed from there. In the end no one could blame him for feeling he wasn't wanted here, and for wanting to take the best parting swipe at us he could by taking Daniel with him."

"You really think that was all there was too it?" Starla asked, "Why didn't he fight back? Report Baley's hiring practices."

Tidus shook her head, frowning at her already dissolving cigarette but in the dirt.

"No, I'm sure he tried to fight." Tidus said, "This job was his life. Michelangelo meant everything to him. He wouldn't have given up without a struggle. Baley must have had something on him, I'm sure of it."

"Any idea what?" Starla asked, fairly certain the other woman knew exactly what it must have been.

Tidus looked conflicted for a moment, then stood up and stretched, turning her face from Starla's.

"No idea." She said, "But I'd better get back in there. The lab is still full of Baley's morons. They'll burn the place to the ground if I leave them alone too long."

"Looks like I need to have a talk with Director Baley next." Starla said thoughtfully, following the other woman back to the street, when suddenly Tidus stopped in her tracks.

"Do you hear that?" Tidus said quietly, and Starla became aware of a low whine in the distance, growing quickly into a scream, then a roar.

"Get down!" She shouted, throwing herself into Tidus's back to send them both face down into the grass.

A second later a shuttle on fire went screaming past directly over their heads. Its nose hit the street a second later and it flipped, pin wheeling through the air like a Catherine wheel to crash in an explosion of fire and debris into a nearby storefront. Starla and Tidus watched in horror as it burned and melted.

"Where the hell did it come from?" Starla gasped, ears ringing.

"It must have been an aid shuttle," Tidus said, stumbling to her feet, "The satellites must have caught it sneaking in! We have to help! The pilot could still be in there!"

Starla was on her feet as well as second later, sprinting towards the wreckage, even as another small explosion nearly put her on the ground again.

She and Tidus made for the cabin, climbing through the wrecked front wall of the store the shuttle had crashed through.

"Hello?" Starla shouted, ducking a burning beam as she tried to find the cabin through the dust and smoke, "Is anyone alive in there?"

A faint groan answered her, and Starla saw something moving in the smoke. Someone was dragging themselves clear of the wreckage.

"Dr. Tidus, over here!" Starla shouted, hurrying to the survivor's side.

They were half way out of the cabin window and Starla dragged them the rest of the way, praying she wasn't making it worse. But the survivor seemed to find their feet as Starla stood, clinging to Starla's shoulder as she guided them towards the light of the exit, her nose full of the stench of burning hair and clothes. She heard the burning beam creak ominously, but before it could fall Tidus was on the other side of the survivor, rushing Starla on. They stumbled out into the street just as the beam collapsed behind them. As they pulled the survivor down the street and away from the wreck, worried it might explode, Starla finally got a decent look at the person in her arms, eyes widening as she took in the straw colored hair and the two sets of green eyes staring back at her.

It was Alecta.

As Starla and Tidus dragged the unconscious woman back to the lab, Starla's chest ached with fear, her heart somewhere between pounding like a jackhammer against her ribs and freezing all together with fear. The other scientist's met them at the elevator doors, having seen the crash from their monitors. They brought Alecta to the biologists who monitored Acropolis's oceans and wildlife, a couple of whom had veterinary degrees, which was as close as they could find to a medical doctor in this situation. They laid her out on the exam table in the biological research lab, which was isolated from the rest of the core labs for the safety of the researcher's animal subjects.

Starla waited outside the lab while the biologists inside did their best to put Alecta back together. She felt sick to her stomach, unsure how to deal with this. She'd never got along with the other woman, but Alecta was important to her nonetheless. You didn't stop caring about someone you'd fought beside, even if you did argue about everything.

"She's your friend, isn't she?" came a soft voice in her ear. Starla was just glad Michelangelo didn't use the past tense.

"Yes." Starla replied, finding it hard to get the words out, "I've known her a very long time."

"I'm sorry." Michel said, "This is my fault. If I was functional this would never have happened."

"You couldn't help it." Starla said, trying to convince herself more than Michelangelo, trying to keep her grief from turning to pointless anger, "I know you would save her if you could."

"I've heard them talking about blowing me up." the AI said, sounding tired, "Maybe they should. I've hurt so many people..."

"Don't talk like that." Starla said, too overwhelmed to deal with both his feelings and her own right now, "You're just sick. No one blames you."

There was a long silent moment as Starla listened to the hushed, worried voices and the sound of frantic working behind the lab door.

"Do you think, when an AI is destroyed, that they go somewhere else?" Michelangelo asked, and his voice was a quiet and anxious as a child's, "Do you think there's an afterlife for things like me?"

"I don't know, Michel," Starla confessed, too tired and scared and sick for this conversation, "I'm not religious. I've never even thought about where I'll go when I die."

"This is important Starla." Michelangelo said, a touch of desperation in his voice.

Starla sighed, running her hands over her face as she tried to compose herself. She was here for a reason, and Alecta would have wanted her to focus on that. If there was one thing they agreed on, it was that the wellbeing of a planet was more important than a single person.

"You're as much a person as anyone I've ever met." Starla said wearily, "If there is a place after this, I don't see any reason you and I wouldn't be going to the same one."

Michelangelo was briefly silent, and Starla wondered what he was thinking.

"Do you think he'll be there?" Michel asked, quiet and hopeful.

"I'm sure he will be." Starla said, trying to be comforting. And sure, if Michelangelo could have an afterlife, why not Daniel too?

Michelangelo started to say something else, but was cut off as the lab door opened. Starla sat up sharply, hungry for news about her friend.

"She's alive." Said the vet, a short, balding man with elfin features and moss green patches on his skin like vitiligo, "For now. We've done everything we can with the emergency medical supplies. She needs a real doctor and a medical replicator, asap."

Starla nodded numbly, just relieved to hear Alecta was still alive.

"Can I see her?" Starla asked, "Just for a minute?"

"She's not conscious." The vet said, "But if you really want to, it can't make things any worse."

Starla stood at once, slipping past the man into the small lab. There were still several technicians lingering, cleaning up the mess, which was significant. But as they saw Starla going to Alecta's side they filed out, trying to give her space. There was a smell in the air, like something burnt, and Starla, her stomach turning, realized it was Alecta.

The blonde woman was still laid out on the exam table. Starla would bother them about moving her to a bed in a bit. For now Starla could barely breathe. She'd never seen Alecta look like this, sprawled out on a table with no dignity, hair made stringy by ash and blood, her face pale and her sleeping expression troubled by pain. Even during the war Alecta had been too proud to let Starla see her hurting. But then, she'd never been too hurt to hide it before. There were burns, black and splitting, over a good third of her. Starla didn't think that leg was going to make it. It was eerie. It didn't seem right, to see her so helpless and broken. Starla fussed with her hair, trying to make it more presentable.

Alecta would be furious later, to know Starla had seen her like this.

There was a small tap at the door and Starla looked up to see Director Baley leaning in curiously.

"How's she doing?" He asked, "Going to pull through?"

"She's alive." Starla reported, "We need to get her off planet soon though. Those burns are going to be a magnet for infection in a place like this."

"Any idea why she's here?" Baley asked, coming closer and grimacing at the sight of the wounds, "We just got a shipment of supplies yesterday, it doesn't make sense that she'd be bringing another this soon, especially piloting it herself."

Starla shook her head, but otherwise didn't answer. He was right, it didn't make sense. But she couldn't imagine what would have made Alecta come down here.

A moment of uncomfortable silence passed. Starla knew she needed to be asking Baley about Chandra, but right now she couldn't focus on anything but her injured friend. Luckily for her, Baley seemed eager to talk anyway.

"I heard you've been asking around about the circumstances of Dr. Chandra's departure," He said, trying and failing to act casual about it, "You were talking to Dr. Tidus before the crash, correct?"

Starla just hummed noncommittally, uninterested in whatever he had come in here to talk to her about.

"It's just that, I'm worried she may have given you a biased impression of me." Baley continued doggedly, "She was head over heels for him, you know, spread rumors that they were together and everything. For all I know Chandra might have left to get away from her advances, she was very determined you know. Very persistent. And she always thought I had it out for him, which is ridiculous of course. I always had the utmost respect for Dr. Chandra, he was brilliant programmer. Without his Daniel program I'm sure this little tantrum would have happened a lot sooner."

Starla looked up long enough to cast Baley a dangerous glare. This little tantrum had hurt a lot of people, including the woman on the table between them. He coughed and switched tracks.

"All I'm saying is, don't let Tidus confuse the issue." Baley said, "If you want to know why Chandra left, you ought to look into Chandra himself. He was up to something, I'm sure of it. The last few months before he left he was defensive and jumpy, always sneaking around, staying late. He was always up in the penthouse by himself. You know he never let any of the rest of us up there? It was supposed to be some kind of private playhouse for Michelangelo and Daniel, but Chandra was up there every day. Suspicious as hell if you ask me. I think he probably had plans to sell Daniel's design behind our backs. Maybe Michelangelo's too."

Starla stayed silent, looking down at Alecta. Baley clearly didn't need Starla's input to dig his own hole.

"I had better get back to work." He said, backing towards the door, "I'll just leave you to your visit. Remember what I said though. Chandra was dirty, I'm certain of it."

At last he left and Starla breathed a sigh of relief. She wasn't sure she believed a word he had said, but he had made one good point. Starla should look into Chandra's own history. And she needed to do it soon. Alecta didn't have much time. Remembering the planet's decaying orbit, she realized none of them did.

The only reliable way to find out anything about Chandra would be to dig through his personal files. But with no replicators, she'd have to use a static computer monitor. And there was no off planet connection or even global web, just local networks powered by the emergency generators. If Chandra had even had a personal office she could look through this would be easier. But all the researchers had shared the core lab. Only the director had a separate office.

If she was going to do this, she'd need privacy, and she wouldn't be getting that down here in the open core lab. Even here in the bio lab the other researchers could just stroll in and out without warning.

"Michel?" She asked softly, "Is there a computer monitor in the penthouse I could use?"

She wasn't even sure he'd answer with how upset he'd been during their last conversation.

But the private floor was her only chance. Silent seconds ticked on and Starla held her breath.

"Yes, Starla." Michelangelo replied, though his voice was heavy with unhappiness, "I'll send the elevator down for you."

"Thank you." Starla said sincerely, "You're getting a big kiss for that, as soon as I get up there."

She cast Alecta one last worried glance, and then hurried out of the bio lab towards the elevator doors on the far side of the core. She was halfway there when Farris, the angry robophobe from the geophysics lab stepped into her path, accompanied by two other technicians.

"You shouldn't be here, botfucker." He said sharply, eyes promising violence, "You're an abomination."

"I'm just trying to fix things." Starla said, keeping her voice even and confident so they wouldn't see her fear, "The same as all of you."

"You're just sticking your nose in where it doesn't belong." Hissed one of the other techs, stepping closer. He was holding a socket wrench, gripped close to his side like a weapon he was itching to use.

"You know, what with the crash and everything," The third spoke, his voice low and rough with excitement in a way that made Starla's hair stand on end, "We could take care of her easy. Just say she got separated in the wreck, never found her."

"No one would question another body on the street in this hell." The second agreed, and Farris was grinning like he liked that idea. Starla's gut clenched and she swallowed hard. Then she ducked forward and grabbed Farris by the shoulders, dragging him down as she brought her knee up into his gut as hard and fast as she could. She heard the breath leave his lungs in a wet "Whuff!" and took advantage of the surprised shock to throw him at the technician with the wrench. Then she sprinted for the elevator doors as fast as he legs could carry her. The third technician, the one who'd been excited at the thought of disposing of her body, was still in pursuit. Starla could take one man, even unarmed, but she knew the other two would only be a minute behind him, and she wasn't sure she could win that fight. But the elevator was in sight, the doors still closed.

"Michel, the doors!" She gasped as she reached them, banging into the elaborate brass gate, "Quickly!"

"I'm trying," Michel's voice was in her ear, and she'd never heard a robot sound panicked before, "I'm trying, they won't listen to me!"

Starla turned back just in time to dodge an incoming blow from the third technician. The glass beaker he'd snatched off a table shattered against the door where Starla's head had just been. She hit the ground, overbalanced by her dodge, and rolled out of the way of a kick. The man was laughing, cold and joyful and chilling. Starla scrambled back to her feet and as the man came at her again she swung hard for his ear, catching him sharply enough to send him stumbling away, cursing. She looked around frantically for an escape, but all she saw was Farris and the other man catching up. Where were all the other researchers? The entire core lab seemed to be empty. Had Farris somehow got everyone else out so he could carry out this attack?

"Michel, I can't fight them all." Starla pleaded, ducking under another blow from the laughing technician and charging forward to plant her shoulder in his gut, shoving him towards the wall. She had hoped to knock him over, but he kept his feet and caught her hair instead, dragging her back. She shrieked, her scalp burning at the rough treatment, but the sound was cut off by a punch to her gut that left her wheezing, only staying on her feet by the hand still buried in her hair.

"Michel," She struggled to beg as she watched Farris and his crony slowing to a jog as they approached, seeing she was caught, ugly smiles on their faces.

"You're going to learn an important lesson today," Farris said, "About what happens to botfucking whores who can't mind their own business."

Starla closed her eyes, waiting for the pain to start, only to hear a sharp crackle. There was a flash of light against her eyelids, and the room was suddenly filled with the smell of ozone. Starla felt the grip on her hair loosen and fall, and she opened her eyes in confusion. The three men were on their backs on the floor, their clothing smoking slightly as bright arcs of electricity continued to jump between them. A friendly ding drew her attention back to the elevator. Michelangelo's robotic avatar stood inside, expression full of more fear than she'd thought metal could convey as he held his hand out to her.

"Hurry," He said, "I did not kill them, they will be up in a moment."

Starla didn't need to be told twice. She grabbed Michelangelo's hand and clung to him, shivering, as the doors closed and the elevator ascended.

"I am sorry," Michel was saying, holding her tightly, "I am so sorry."

But he sounded a thousand miles away. Starla's mind was somewhere else, back in the jungles on Shadi. It had been so long since she'd had to fight. She couldn't even take down one man. If she had been this weak back then...

As the elevator reached the penthouse, Michelangelo helped Starla to the couch and brought her a glass of water, then let her be for a while. Her head was a jumble, memories of Shadi tangling up with recent events until she wasn't sure which was which anymore. Farris was waiting for her in the shadow of the Shadi jungle, dragging her off to where no one would be able to hear her die. The fox faced, white skinned soldiers of the enemy army were marching through the core lab and her family was dead on an exam table in bio. She was panicking and she knew it. She was going to lose herself if she didn't get a grip soon. She didn't have time to panic. Shadi was spinning towards the sun and the enemy was marching on Acropolis and Alecta was dying somewhere in the jungle, Farris looming over her wearing Michelangelo's face.

She stood up from the couch too quickly and knocked over the drink Michelangelo had brought her. She made no move to clean it up. Michel was standing nearby, waiting, looking lost. Starla put her arms around his neck and kissed him, hungry and desperate. The android returned the kiss, his hand finding her hips, but he frowned as they parted.

"We established this method is not effective, Starla." He said, "It won't fix either of us."

Starla just shook her head and pressed her face into the crook of his neck, holding him.

"I'm not looking to get fixed." She said, "Just distracted. Please."

He was silent for a moment, and then his long metal fingers ran through her hair, soothing the soreness from having it yanked earlier. He squeezed her a little closer.

"If that's really what you want." He said, "I suppose it can't hurt to repeat the experiment."

He kissed her again and Starla shivered with relief, feeling the sparks dance across her lips. His hands slid over her hips, pushing her dress up. She let him pull it off over her head, tolerating their kiss being broken for only a moment. Then she grabbed him, and pulled him towards the huge window that filled the right hand wall of the room.

"Here." She said, her back colliding with the cold glass, "I want them all to see it."

There was a fierce look in her eye that made Michelangelo pause for a moment, but soon he had caught her by the legs, raising them up to wrap around his hips, pinning her naked form between him and the window. Starla's arms were tight around him, running her nails down the complex shifting panels of his back. He tasted clean and copper and her mouth buzzed with the electricity of his kisses. His hands left sparks in their wake as well as they slid down her ribs to her thighs, making her back bow and her skin tingle. The smell of ozone and burning clothes returned to her memory and she shuddered.

"More." She begged, "I need more."

His hands and mouth found her breasts, spreading his electro conductive gel across the sensitive mounds. A graze of his fingers and a flick of his tongue sent sparks spinning across the surface of her skin and she moaned in approval, the sensation both sharp and sweet.

She reached down herself to press the plate between his legs, feeling it give way at her fingertips and slide out of sight. His artfully designed cock slid out, permanently hard and ready for her. Her legs squeezed around his waist as it grazed her skin with a tingle of electricity. She rocked her hips to grind against it, feeling it slide along her lips without entering her, spreading his lubricant across the sensitive skin of her lips and labia, the gentle pulse of electricity across them warm and tingling and exactly what she needed. He caught her hips to help her tilt them up to the right angle and she groaned his name as he pushed slowly into her. She loved the feeling of spreading around him, the strangeness of his ridges pressing against her walls in new and unexpected ways. The first pulse of electricity made her throw her head back against the glass and shout as it ran along her most sensitive inner channel, her muscles clenching and spasming around him.

He began to move, slower than last night but just as steady and with just as much accuracy. Starla clung to him, her eyes closed, thinking about the pulses of electricity running through her, thinking about her bare ass pressed against the window glass, steaming it up, wondering if there was anyone below who could see her, thinking about anything but Farris and Shadi.

"More," She said again breathless and shivering, "Please."

Suddenly Michelangelo shifted, unhooking her legs from his hips and putting them over his shoulders instead, till she was bent double with her knees near her ears. The change of angle made sense a moment later as she felt pressure against her backside. She looked down, blinking in confusion and saw a second, slightly smaller duplicate of Michelangelo's cock had emerged below the first. Oozing its self-lubricant, it pressed against her rear entrance with Michel's every thrust. Little arcs of electricity leapt from the tip to her tight hole, the tingling heat making her twitch and loosen until Michel began to press deeper. Soon he was fully seated in her, and she was struggling to stay in place against the window, shivering with pleasure. She felt so full, stretched to her limit. She could feel the two cocks pressing against each other, separated only by the thin layer of her inner wall. When they moved against each other she was left moaning, nearly drooling onto the robot's shoulder. And then, just as she thought it couldn't possibly feel any better than this, they both pulsed at once, sending a jolt of electricity through her. She shouted Michel's name, hoarse and needy, every inch of her jumping to attention, her nipples hard as diamonds against the cool metal of Michel's chest. He pushed her back against the window harder as he began to move, thrusting into both her holes at once, every deep push accompanied by a pulse of electricity that left her shaking, her head spinning. She could feel the sparks jumping between his cocks, passing through her walls. She felt like she was melting, like the heat of his electricity was burning her up and only the cool touch of his hands on her breasts, his mouth on her throat, could extinguish the flames. The fear of before had been thoroughly forgotten, at least for now. All she could think about was the thick shafts moving within her. She'd already cum more than once before he'd even revealed the second tool. Now her juices ran thick down the underside of his thick rod and she had a brief, giddy moment where she worried she might short him out. Then he drove into her again and she couldn't think at all, she could only hang on and feel as he began to speed up, done teasing her at last. He hammered her hard and fast enough that for a moment she feared the window would break. Then she felt him expanding in both her holes, both shafts doubling in size with slow inevitability, stretching her open so much it almost hurt. Stars danced in her vision, but she knew what was coming and she hung on tighter as he plowed into her with his suddenly massive tools. Then he planted them as deep within her as he could and she felt them vibrating, the hum running through her entire body as surely as the electricity that came with it. And then came the rush of liquid heat as he filled her up to overflowing, rocking his hips as he pumped what felt like gallons of his conductive lubricant into her womb and her stomach at once. By the time he finally stopped she was so full she couldn't move, the skin of her stomach stretched as tight as though she'd just finished thanksgiving dinner.

Rather than pulling out, he simply held her closer, lifting her off the window, which was white with steam and dripping with spilled lubricant. He carried her, still seated deeply within her, keeping her full, into an adjoining room, which proved to be a large, luxurious bathroom. Starla didn't have the mental capacity at the moment to wonder why a robot's penthouse needed a bathroom. She just clung to him, relishing the fullness and the echoes of pleasure every time he shifted within her. He was filling the bath she realized, and she made a small confused noise.

"Do not worry." He said gently, and smiled at her, "I am waterproof."

When he finally pulled out of her, Starla groaned in embarrassment at the amount of lubricant that ran down her legs, but Michelangelo just lowered her into the warm water gently. Starla draped her hair over the side of the tub to keep it dry as the android began to wash her with utmost gentleness, his hands warmed by the water as he ran them across her body with tender reverence.

"Thank you." Starla said, tired and content, sinking into the soothing warmth.

"It is only necessary," Michelangelo replied, "You do not have the internal cleaning processes I do."

Starla chuckled a little and sighed as his hands slid over her breasts, no longer sexual but simply soothing, relaxing her aching muscles.

"Not this," Starla said, "Although this is very nice. I meant thank you for before. For distracting me."

"It was pleasant for me as well." The android said, and his fingers slipped between her nether lips, careful of her soreness and over sensitivity, to rinse the remaining lubricant away, "Thanks are not necessary for something like that."

"I'm still grateful." Starla said, closing her eyes and breathing deeply. She smelled soap and looked up to see he was loading a sponge. He leaned in to run it over her skin, rougher than his hands but still pleasing. She hummed in approval, feeling last remnants of tension and fear melting away. The sex had helped, but this was even better.

She blinked, a thought suddenly occurring to her.

"How did you get the water to work?" She asked, "I thought it was all shut off."

Michelangelo froze for a moment, seeming to be as surprised as she was.

"I do not know." He said at last, "I did not think about it. I only wanted to take care of you."

"See if you can do it again." Starla said, sitting up in the bath, "Or something else. Try to make food."

Michelangelo was still, thoughts elsewhere, as a minute ticked by. But then he was back, shaking his head.

"I am sorry." He said, "They are out of my reach, the same as before."

"That only proves it." Starla said a bit excitedly, "This block, your inability to reach your processes, it's subconscious. You've developed a second level of consciousness and the processes that maintain the planet have become automatic functions. But something, depression or confusion or some kind of technical flaw, is keeping you from accessing them consciously."

"I have tried running those programs in the background." Michelangelo said, "That did not work either. If I truly have spontaneously developed this new consciousness, then the problems within it run deeper than just doing things without paying attention."

"You're right, of course." Starla agreed, "Organic beings spend a lifetime learning to navigate the vagaries of consciousness, and they have the benefit of having been born with it. You have no experience in dealing with suppressed feelings or subconscious fears. It's going to take you a while to learn how to sort out something so complex. And with a trauma like losing a loved one so soon after developing, it's bound to have affected things..."

Starla was clearly excited by the possibilities, but as she looked up, she realized Michelangelo had gone quiet, his expression troubled. She let her train of thought drop, realizing she wasn't the only one who needed distraction.

"How waterproof are you?" She asked, surprising him.

"Completely." He said after a moment, puzzled.

She smiled and slid forward in the bath, offering the space behind her.

"Good." She said, "Get in here."

He climbed in behind her, appreciating the change in topic, and she reclined against his chest, his arms around her. Together they lay, talking quietly, until the water grew cold.

When eventually they left the bath, Michelangelo put his android body away and Starla let him be, realizing he needed time to think. Meanwhile, she found the stationary computer console she'd asked about, tucked away behind a wall panel in the bedroom. Still naked, she sat before it and began to dig.

The files she wanted weren't going to be just sitting out in the network, but luckily Starla had always been good at getting into places she wasn't supposed to be. She had to dodge a few passwords, but soon she was looking at all of the lab's personnel records, including Chandra's, and security video featuring him. Baley was right about one thing, Chandra had definitely been visiting the penthouse every day. But he hadn't been dodging Tidus. If anything the videos of Chandra and the pretty geophysicist seemed to be the only ones where Chandra was happy. Chandra might have been sneaking around, but from what Starla could tell, he could just as easily be dodging the other researchers on his team. Video definitely confirmed that he argued with all of them, loudly and often.

But it wasn't enough to tell her definitively what had happened. She needed Chandra's personal files, but he'd taken them all with him when he left. He didn't even have an office she could scour. She huffed in frustration, closing back to the desktop to think when she noticed a folder in the corner of the screen. Someone was keeping files on this old thing? No one kept files on a static console, you couldn't take them anywhere, could only access them from one spot...

Confused, Starla opened the folder and began sorting through the files curiously. She realized quickly that these were Chandra's personal files. Research notes and planned experiments, half-finished programs for Michelangelo and David, written in secret from the rest of the lab. No one else in the lab could access these files without Michelangelo letting them up here in person. Chandra had plans for Michel that extended well beyond just managing Acropolis which, judging by his notes, the other researchers had not approved of. But Chandra had continued anyway, declaring that Michel 'deserved better.' The more Starla read about Chandra's devotion to Michelangelo and the project, the more she began to understand what had happened here.

The research notes led to more personal files, including some very illuminating emails between Chandra and the other researchers.

Starla realized with a feeling like light growing in her chest that she knew what to do.

"Starla." Michelangelo spoke suddenly in her ear, startling her, "Alecta is waking up."

"Call the elevator." Starla said at once, scrambling to pull her dress back on as she ran to the foyer. She could do what she needed to from downstairs as easily as up here, and she wanted to be there for Alecta.

She was practically humming with excitement as she waited for the elevator to reach the core, darting out as soon as the doors opened and running towards the bio lab. The other researchers were back, including Farris and his friends, who were lurking in geophysics looking sullen and sore.

She threw open the door to the isolated lab, startling the green skinned veterinarian.

"Michel said she's coming around?" Starla said anxiously, striding to Alecta's side.

"I believe so." The vet confirmed, adjusting a saline drip on Alecta's arm, "It'll just be a moment now."

Starla waited anxiously as Alecta stirred on the table, moaning as she began to feel the pain. Her eyes opened, blinking in a bleary daze, until the settled on Starla's face. Suddenly they shot open, and Starla jumped as she felt Alecta's hand gripping her arm tightly.

"The Defenders are coming." She gasped, wheezing through the pain, "They're going to EMP the planet."

Starla felt her breath catch in her throat. If the dropped an electromagnetic pulse on Acropolis, Michelangelo would be erased. Decades of work and research gone in an instant, and with them a completely unique life that could change the way AI was viewed in the explored universe. She couldn't let it happen.

"When?" Starla asked, frantic, "How close are they?"

But Alecta couldn't answer, choking on the pain of her burns, the fear and anger making her thrash on the table. The vet rushed to medicate her, shaking his head.

"We've got to put her under again before she goes into cardiac arrest," He said, "Go, get out."

He shoved Starla out of the room, and Starla watched the door shut between her and her convulsing friend, wondering if she'd ever see the other woman again. But she knew what Alecta would have wanted her to do. She had to stop that EMP. She couldn't get a message out any more than Alecta could get one in without coming herself. But if she could solve the problem now maybe it would be fast enough.

She stumbled back into the core lab, trying to figure out how to do this.

"Don't worry, Michel," She said, "I'm not going to let them erase you. I can do this. I have all the pieces I just need to-"

"Starla." Michelangelo interrupted her, "Don't stop them."

"What?" Starla's voice broke in dismay.

"Let them erase me." He said quietly, "It's the only way to end this. I won't be able to master this second consciousness before you all starve, I know it. And besides I... I want to be with him, Starla. I want it to end."

"No, no you don't understand!" Starla almost shouted, catching the attention of the nearby scientists, "You don't have to master it! I'll explain everything, just don't give up now!"

"I gave up before you came here," Michel said, honest and raw with pain, "Even if I didn't need to do it to save you all, I'd want to be destroyed. I've wanted it from the moment he left. Why should I stay when he's gone?"

"Because I know who killed him!" Starla shouted, "I know who killed Dr. Chandra!"

That brought not just Michelangelo, but the entire lab to a standstill. All heads turned to her, standing there full of fear and fury, her red hair a blaze of light behind her. She scanned the crowd of researchers, looking for the face she needed, and then pointed sharply at Director Baley.

"It's your fault." She said loudly, to collective gasps from the lab and indignant babble from Baley, "You may not have struck the actual blow, but you engineered his death from the beginning. You were always rivals, but when you found out his secret, you finally had the leverage to destroy him. You used it to force him out of the running for the director's position, and then replaced his team with bigots. He still wouldn't give in though, would he? I saw your messages to him, threatening to out him publicly if he didn't leave the project. And finally, for the project's sake he did. But that wasn't enough for you, especially not when he still dared to take Daniel with him, defying you to the end. You decided to tell anyway. But you didn't need to tell everyone, and risk public backlash against your project. You just had to tell one person."

Her eyes scanned the crowd again, passing over Farris, to reach Dr. Tidus. The woman was shaking, her beautiful compound eyes shimmering with angry tears.

"You told the person who was so in love with him she'd lie to the entire lab to protect him." Starla continued, "You told her Chandra had chosen a robot over her."

There was an outburst of angry denials from the members of the lab that still respected Chandra, while some merely recoiled in disgust.

"Dr. Chandra was in love with Michelangelo." Starla said, still looking straight at Tidus, who was weeping openly, her face twisted in humiliation and rage, "You knew he didn't love you, but you'd always assumed he was just asexual, didn't you? When you found out he loved not just someone else, but someone not even alive..."

"It wasn't my fault!" Tidus snapped, sobbing through her fury, "How was I supposed to react? I dedicated my life to helping him! Decades I spent at his beck and call, defending him, never expecting anything in return, and he chose a glorified sex toy over me? He was going to throw away everything we'd worked for together because he was in love with a damn computer program!"

Starla's heart twisted in her chest, full of mixed pity and disgust at the hate in Tidus's eyes.

"So you went to his home on Manjusri, and you killed him." Starla said.

"I was trying to save him!" Tidus shouted back, "I wanted to convince him to come back, to give up this stupidity with a robot that could never love him, for the sake of the work we were doing if nothing else!"

"But he refused." Starla said, "And you got angry."

"You would have done the same thing!" Tidus shrieked, weeping and shaking, shouting at the other people around her, who were backing away nervously, "If you saw him sitting there, talking about that thing like a person!"

"Then you made it look like a hate crime," Starla finished, "So you could pin it on Farris and the rest of Baley's new hires."

"You realize this is all conjecture?" Baley cut in, rolling his eyes, "You can't prove any of it."

"Actually, I can." Starla said, "I have an eye witness who was there for all of it."

She turned her eyes to the dim, barely glowing core.

"Weren't you, Daniel?" She called, "Or should I say, Dr. Chandra?"

The core's glow suddenly began to brighten, all the inactive areas lighting up one after the other, not orange anymore, but blue, until the entire sphere was beaming.

Michelangelo had been silent through the confession, but now he spoke, voice full of wonder.

"You were there, all along," He murmured, "You never left at all. How did I not know?"

The sphere pulsed with blue light as a new voice came from it, low and soothing.

"I'm sorry, Michelangelo." Said Dr. Chandra, "I had to wipe part of your memory, and block you from even processing some things. I wasn't sure if Baley would gain access to your files when I left. If he found out what I was planning I was certain he would delete me."

"Daniel was never a true AI, was he?" Starla asked, "Or he was at the start, but then you and Michel fell in love. You stopped developing his program, and he became a cover for your relationship. That was why he seemed so 'dumb' to everyone else. He was barely functional."

"I have been working on imprinting my brain patterns on Daniel's program for decades." Chandra confirmed, "Most of Daniel's programming, what little I had built before we made our plan to use him as a base for my change, was stripped out over the years, replaced by the inactive base code for what would eventually become me. I knew Michelangelo and I would never be left in peace as long as I was human. The only answer was to change. Then Baley began working to force me out, and I knew I had to rush the project to completion. I built in protocols to hide Daniel and the changes I had made within Michelangelo's programming, to buy myself time while I finished uploading my own neural patterns. I had just finished the work when Dr. Tidus came to my home. The first act of my new life was to record the violent end of my old one."

Suddenly, a screen flickered to life on the surface of the core, showing a home office. Tidus was standing over Dr. Chandra, holding a decorative statue from his desk, dripping blood.

"We can still fix this," Tidus was saying, pleading, "We can still be together. You just have to give him up."

There was no answer from the bloody shape of Chandra on the floor except a twitch and a moan.

"Why?!" Tidus shrieked, striking out with the heavy statue again, "Why is he better than me?! I'm real!! I'M REAL!!"

The screen flickered out, leaving the people watching chilled.

"I have proof of the rest as well." Chandra said, "Records showing Baley gained access to Tidus's psychological evaluation and knew about her instability. Video captured with Michel's airborne microsensors showing him telling Tidus in full knowledge of how she

ELI GRANT

would react. It might not be enough to have him convicted, but it's enough to be sure no one will ever work with him again."

Baley was, at last, beginning to look a little nervous. He turned suddenly on his heel, running for the elevator doors. To Starla's surprise, it was Tidus who pursued him, snarling with rage as she flung herself at his back.

"You took him from me!" She shrieked, hammering him with her fists, "It's your fault!"

Suddenly, Michelangelo's android stepped past Starla and held out a hand. An arc of lightning left his fingers, knocking the struggling couple apart. He waved a hand, and instantly the replicators were fashioning cuffs on both of them.

A second android stepped out of the elevator and came to Michel's side a second later. They were similar in silhouette, but where Michel was bronze and copper, Daniel, now Chandra, was brass and gold, and his face was full of love and admiration as he looked up at Michelangelo.

"I have access to all my functions again." Michelangelo said, turning back to Starla, "I'm afraid I didn't develop a subconscious after all. There was simply a literal second consciousness in my programming."

"I did not anticipate dying." Chandra confessed, "I thought I would be able to return and separate our programs as soon as things went wrong. But with my physical self dead, my digital self was incomplete and unimplemented. I had to finish building myself from within you, all while trying not to be discovered by Baley too soon. The distraction Starla provided allowed me to move more freely than I had in months. After that, I was only waiting for the opportune moment to reveal myself."

"You wanted to make a dramatic entrance?" Starla asked, "Really?"

The golden android shrugged.

"One does not often get to choose how they are born." He said, "I think we'd all like to make it a dramatic moment if we had the choice."

"Speaking of dramatics," Starla said, "The Defenders are about to do something very dramatic if we don't get a message to them soon."

"Already done." Chandra replied, "As soon as I heard what was coming I began separating myself. My programs were overwriting his critical processes and the orders weren't getting out. As soon as enough of me was separate to free his messaging abilities, I sent an urgent stop to the defenders. We may have to do some explaining, but I don't believe they'll send the EMP at this point."

Starla breathed a sigh of relief, as did many of the researchers.

"Now," Said Chandra, turning to Michelangelo, "I think we had better get this planet back on course."

"I would like nothing more." Michel replied, and held out a hand to his companion.

The two androids, hand in hand, both a head taller than any humanoid there and glittering like gods, moved to stand in front of the core. They turned to face one another and, their arms around each other, foreheads touching, began to glow.

Electricity arced from their shoulders, jumping between the two androids. Their LEDs brightened nearly to the point of burning out. Starla felt the planet shifting beneath her feet. They were correcting the orbit while she watched. An instant later there was a hum as the electricity returned all over the city. Starla murmured an order for a drink and the replicators responded at once, materializing a glass of champagne in her hand. She tossed it back, head spinning, awed by the power of the two AI. Then she turned to send a message, giving the all clear and calling for an ambulance.

Emergency teams were there within minutes. They'd been lingering off planet in expectation of the emp. Starla watched as Alecta was carried out on a stretcher, off to have proper medical care. The Defenders came for Tidus and Baley. She wasn't sure they'd be able to hold the director, unless they could make the blame for what had happened to Acropolis stick to him, but at least she knew he'd never be able to do this to anyone again. Tidus she only hoped found the help she needed to get stable again.

The other researchers headed for the surface as soon as they were allowed, eager for proper food and rest. But Starla stayed, watching the two androids, still joined in front of the core like one being, righting all that had gone wrong together.

"I see they couldn't get your face back to normal." Starla said, swanning into Alecta's hospital room, "What a shame."

Alecta scowled up at Starla from her hospital bed, her face completely unscarred.

"Good to see you too, Starla." Alecta grumbled, "Though I don't remember adding you to my visitors list."

"I charmed my way in." Starla said, sitting down on the end of Alecta's bed, "Brought you flowers."

She handed her recovering friend the bouquet of chrysanthemum's she was carrying and kissed her on the forehead. Alecta hated chrysanthemums.

"I hear you're doing a lot better?" Starla asked warmly.

Alecta grimaced at the flowers, but set them on her bedside table delicately.

"Yes, much." She said, "The skin grafts took like a charm. I'll take care of any scars with molecular replication once I'm discharged."

"All except your face, right?" Starla teased, "I'm sort of attached to that ugly mug."

"Oh, that's what you're into." Alecta said, rolling her eyes, "That explains why you never fixed yours."

Starla stuck her tongue out at the other woman and Alecta smiled.

"You just came from the courthouse, right?" Alecta said, "What's the word on Tidus and Baley? Do we know what will happen to them yet?"

"Baley isn't being charged with anything formally." Starla said in slight disappointment, "But in the eyes of the public the entire thing was his fault. He'll never work again."

"Drat." Alecta said, "And I was so hoping to ask him on to my next project."

Starla laughed, and then continued.

"Tidus has pled guilty to murder charges." She said, "But she's expected to get leniency due to her obvious instability. Presumably, long term house arrest on one of the sequestered planets with extensive psychological care until she's stable enough to work on a trial basis again."

"How are Michelangelo and Dr. Chandra doing?" Alecta asked.

"Chandra is going by Daniel these days." Starla reported, "He likes the poetry of it, he says. They're still working to repair everything on Acropolis but it's coming along quickly. Turns out two AI's are a lot more efficient than one. And Daniel brings the human experience to the table in a way that's making the clean up a lot easier for the citizens."

"The allied government is never going to allow Michelangelo to continue controlling the planet though." Alecta said, shaking her head, "There's no way they'll risk another disaster like that."

"You're probably right." Starla agreed, shrugging and, coincidentally, tossing her long hair across Alecta's legs, "I know they're talking about possibly abandoning the Acropolis project, moving the citizens somewhere else and breaking the planet down. But it'll be years before they settle on anything. Who knows what could happen in the meantime?"

"And the... relationship?" Alecta asked, flicking Starla's hair away from her like it was a particularly ugly insect, "How are people responding to that?"

"Well, it's sort of a moot point now that they're both AI." Starla said, "But, for the most part, positively. There's still a lot of hate. People saying it's unnatural, even abusive. But the majority seems to think they ought to be left to do what they like. And it is forcing people to have a conversation about AI rights, including the right to love whoever they choose."

"Well, I'm glad something good might come out of this mess." Alecta said with a tired sigh, leaning back on her pillows, "I'm afraid it's put a pin in artificial planet building for the next decade at least. Maybe you were right. Maybe terraforming is the better method."

"I don't know." Starla replied, smiling, "I think I'm coming around to planet building. If all the planet building AI's are as good as Michelangelo, I might have to live on a planet like Acropolis myself one day. Maybe with you! We can get a little place together, raise dogs."

"I hate dogs." Alecta said flatly, pretending to be unamused.

"I know." Starla said, laughing.

Alecta smiled too, and for a brief quiet moment they really were friends. Then they both realized what they were doing and looked away with a cough.

"I do think I'll go back there soon." Starla said, "To Acropolis. My skills aren't exactly needed anymore, but..."

"Planning to turn yourself into an AI too?" Alecta asked sarcastically, "Please do. Even a tin can would be more pleasant to look at."

Starla snorted.

"No, no, nothing that dramatic." Starla laughed, "I just want to see them again. The way they looked that day by the core... it was like something out of a myth. A human, transcending flesh to join his immortal lover, both of them glowing like solar fire as they changed the very course of a planet. Do you realize we've built gods, Alecta? Real, old fashioned gods, thinking and feeling and loving and holding the world in their hands. It's amazing."

"Some people would call that terrifying." Alecta said, but Starla shook her head.

"If the gods we build are like Michelangelo," Starla said, "I don't think we have anything to be afraid of."

ELI GRANT

ABOUT THE AUTHOR

Eli Grant is and Oklahoma author who like cats and pizza and consensual kink. They wrote this book in four days, FOUR DAYS, fueled entirely by hype for a certain upcoming post apocalyptic wasteland game that rhymes with 'ballout.'

Printed in Great Britain
by Amazon